This book

belongs to:

●●●●●●●●●●●●●●●●●●●●●●●●●●●●●●●●●●●●●●

●●●●●●●●●●●●●●●●●●●●●●●●●●●●●●●●●●●●●●

The Flying Pig

and other stories

Written by
NICOLA BAXTER

Illustrated by
SASCHA LIPSCOMB

p

This is a Parragon Book
This edition published in 2002

Parragon
Queen Street House
4 Queen Street
Bath BA1 1HE, UK

Copyright © Parragon 2000

ISBN 0-75259-499-0

Produced for Parragon by
Nicola Baxter

Designed by Amanda Hawkes
Cover designed by Gemma Hornsby
Cover illustrated by Andrew Everitt- Stewart

Printed in Italy

Contents

The
Flying Pig

Many pigs are happy with a normal, snuffling, munching kind of life. They may moan about the size of their dinners. They may wish they had more wallowing time. But on the whole they are happy being pigs.

Puggle wasn't like that. Even as a piglet he yearned for something more. When his father introduced him, with a show of natural piggy pride, to the proper techniques for rootling out turnips, Puggle shook his little pink head.

"I might get my nose dirty," he said.

Puggle's father paused. He could hardly believe his ears. I mean, pigs *like* getting dirty, don't they? Nose, tummies, trotters and tails are regularly covered in mud. By comparison, rootling for turnips is a clean and tidy job. The older pig decided that he simply hadn't made himself clear.

"You see, son," he said, raising his voice a little and talking very slowly, "turnips are good to eat. Mmmm! Yummy! And in order to get them out of the ground, you have to shovel about with your snout, like this. Mmmnnfffmmm! See? It's not unpleasant. It's fun! It's something pigs are good at. Rootling, that is. Now, you have a go."

"No, thank you," said Puggle. He always had been a polite little pig.

Mr. Pig tried again. "It's not a case of 'No, thank you,' Puggle," he said, a little more sharply. "This is something that *all* pigs do. And you will do it too. In fact, you will do it now. Get rootling!"

Puggle knew the voice of command when he heard it, so he rootled. But he really cannot be said to have enjoyed it. And turnips have never been his favourite food from that day to this.

A very similar thing happened when Mrs. Pig tried to teach her son how to wallow really effectively in not-quite-wet-enough mud.

"You have to wiggle on your back a bit more," she explained, "which you don't have to do if the mud is really slurpy. Look, like this!"

And she wallowed very well.

"Now it's your turn, Puggle," she smiled. "This will be a real treat."

"But Puggle looked dubiously down at the puddle in front of his trotters.

"Must I?" he asked. "It doesn't seem very dignified, somehow."

"Dignified? Dignified? What on earth are you talking about?" squeaked his mother. "Wallowing is very dignified —for a pig. Who have you been talking to?"

Both Mr. and Mrs. Pig had a great fear of Undesirable Influences. By this they chiefly meant the sheep out in the meadow, who had nothing to do all day but gossip and who were quite likely to fill a young pig's head full of nonsense. Now that Mrs. Pig came to think about it, she felt sure that was what had happened. After all, sheep are always terribly nervous about getting their coats dirty. She gave her son a piece of her mind on the subject of sheep and their silliness and told him to run away and play so that she could wallow in peace.

Puggle was happy to escape into the farmyard. The sooner he could get back to his experiments, the better.

Yes, the reason that Puggle was not interested in rootling or wallowing was because he was *very* interested in flying. Ever since he had first looked up and seen the blue sky full of fluffy white clouds, he had longed to fly.

Later, when he was still a tiny piglet squiggling in the straw, he had been almost unbearably excited by the sight of a flock of swallows flying overhead. So animals could fly too! He couldn't wait to start flying himself.

Almost as soon as he could walk, Puggle was ready to fly. Except, of course, that there was a problem. He wasn't ready. No pig was ready.

"Mother," he asked one day, "when will my wings grow?"

Mrs. Pig heard "wings" but thought "tusks". The question didn't make any sense otherwise.

"You need to be a bit older, Puggle," she said, "and even then, not all pigs grow tusks. You must be patient."

Puggle was patient—for a week or two. Then he asked the question again. This time, there wasn't any doubt. Mrs. Pig frowned and paused in her munching.

"Wings? What wings?" she said. "Honestly, Puggle, you do have some extraordinary ideas. Pigs don't have wings, sweetheart."

"What, never ever?" asked Puggle. "Never, ever, ever?"

"Not ever," said Mrs. Pig firmly. "It's a silly idea, Puggle. Pigs are too ... er ... portly to fly. A nicely rounded pig couldn't get off the ground under his own steam however many wings he had."

Puggle was shattered. He had assumed that it was only a matter of time before he too could be soaring through the blue. It seemed he would have to explore other avenues.

A few days later, Puggle was lying miserably under a tree, when he happened to overhear a mother blackbird teaching her little ones how to fly. This was news to Puggle.

He had assumed that flying came naturally to a creature with wings. But as he listened to the blackbird mother giving careful instructions to her brood, he felt hope rising within him once again. If bird-brained blackbirds could learn to fly, surely a super-intelligent pig could do it, given enough thought and practice.

There followed several very painful days during which Puggle tried to launch himself off higher and higher objects. The feed trough incident only jolted his front trotters. The sty wall incident left him with a badly bumped bottom.

The sty roof attempt could have been much more serious, but it was luckily an excellent day for wallowing, and the many pigs who were doing so were quite plump and squashy—ideal material on which to land. Even so, Puggle's pride was badly dented and several elderly pigs took to their beds, suffering from shock.

Puggle thought long and hard about jumping from the tree where the baby birds had been practising. He certainly had the courage to try it, but he soon found that trotters were not ideal for climbing tree trunks. Once again, Puggle felt that his dreams had been crushed. He lay under the tree and moaned softly to himself (and that was only partly because of the badly bumped bottom).

Once again, it was a chance event that gave Puggle hope. High overhead, he heard a droning sound. It grew louder and louder and louder. A squirrel who lived in the trunk of the tree came hurtling through the branches, desperate to get back into her hole.

"What is it?" yelled Puggle, for the noise overhead was very loud now.

"It's an aeroplane," shouted the squirrel. "Haven't you ever seen one before? They're a real nuisance, especially when I'm trying to get my little ones to sleep. I can hardly hear myself think!"

Puggle waited a moment or two for the noise to die away, then he turned to the squirrel, who was preparing to leap off up the tree again, and begged for more information.

"But what is it?" he asked. "I mean, what is an aeroplane? I know that it flies and it makes a lot of noise. Is it an animal? Does it do anything else? Does it ever come to land?"

"I'm not completely sure," confessed the squirrel, anxious to be gone. "I don't think it's an animal. I think it's a machine, like a car. And I don't think it ever does land. I've never seen one on the ground. I think it drones about up there all the time."

But when the squirrel had gone, and Puggle had a chance to think, he felt more optimistic once again. You see, pigs are a lot cleverer than squirrels, and the squirrel had said that an aeroplane was like a car. Puggle knew that cars carried people. Wasn't it possible that aeroplanes carried people as well, only through the air instead of along the ground?

The more Puggle thought about it, the more sure he felt that this was the case. A few days later, his suspicions were confirmed when one of the farm children left a library book out on the grass. Puggle had nibbled the cover and chewed a cou-

ple of pages before he noticed that the pictures in the book were all of flying

machines. And the machines definitely
had people in them. Certainly, they were
strange people, with helmets and scarves
and huge goggly eyes, but then people
were strange anyway, in pig terms. Puggle
looked very carefully at the pictures and
was very sorry about the pages that were
now inside him. He wished he could read
the black squiggles. Nevertheless, Puggle
went to sleep that night with a head

buzzing with ideas. For the first time in a long while, flying seemed a real possibility.

The next morning, Puggle set to work to build his flying machine. It's surprising what you can find lying in the back of a barn if you look hard enough. Pretty soon, Puggle had assembled a large crate, a bicycle wheel, a plank of wood and lots of bits of binder twine to fix everything together. Trotters are not ideal for tying knots, but snouts are pretty good, so by the end of the day, Puggle had something that looked very like a plane.

At least, it had a cockpit and wings, and the bicycle wheel on the front looked a little bit like a propeller.

Puggle knew that it would be wise to get a good night's sleep before starting on his adventure. He wasn't, for one thing, quite sure how easy night flying was. But halfway to his sty, he turned around. This was too exciting to wait. If he was going to fly, he must do it now!

As the sun set behind the far fields, Puggle climbed into his flying machine. He thought hard about flying, but nothing happened. He peered over the edge of the cockpit but found he was still very near the ground. Nearer, in fact, than very near. As near as you can get. Once again, Puggle paused for thought.

Of course! A machine needed to make noise to work. Certainly the farmer's car and tractors made a terrible noise, and now he came to think of it, the aeroplane had made a truly deafening din.

"Brrrrrrrrrrmmmmmm!" said Puggle. "Brrrrrmm! Brrrmm! BRRRRMMM!"

But nothing happened. The plane didn't so much as jiggle. It was as earth-bound as a pig. And the pig on board was feeling his heart sink to his trotters once again. Sadly, he climbed out and set off for the sty.

Now Puggle was a fortunate young pig in many ways, and not only because he had such an enquiring mind. He also happened to be a particularly fine-looking pig, which is not surprising when you consider that both his parents had won prizes at the County Show.

A few days later, the farmer gave Puggle a very thorough wash (including parts he didn't even know he had) and brushed his trotters until they shone. Then he loaded the young pig, together with a sheep who looked as if she had been to the hairdresser's and a duck with astonishingly white feathers, into the back of his truck and set off for the local show ground. He felt pretty sure that Puggle at least would win a rosette.

Puggle rather enjoyed his wash and brush up. He liked the idea of seeing somewhere new, too. After all, it would keep his mind off the disappointments in his flying career.

Puggle did, indeed, do very well at the show. He won first prize and had a great many ladies in hats and men with monocles cooing over him. But later in the afternoon, while the judges were looking at the sheep, Puggle became rather bored. He lifted the latch of his crate with his clever little snout and set off to explore the show ground. He might have aroused some comment from the crowd if at that moment everyone had not been staring at the sky. A familiar noise was coming louder and louder above the throng.

Puggle couldn't see a thing among all the legs of the crowd. He climbed up on to a bale of straw and could hardly believe his eyes. There was a flying machine, flying low enough for him to be sure, yes, that there was a person inside. And the machine was looping-the-loop and doing all kinds of acrobatic stunts. Puggle's heart was thudding as the plane came in to land to the applause of the crowd. As the pilot jumped out on to the field, the spectators surged forward to meet him.

Why did no one notice a little pink shape flashing across the field? Why did no one notice when the engine of the plane throbbed into life again? Even when the plane began to move forward, slowly at first and then faster and faster, no one shouted. It was only when Puggle pulled the throttle right back and the engines roared into the loudest of life that the pilot, busy autographing programmes, yelled out, "My plane!"

It was too late. Puggle grinned and waved a careless trotter to the people who were getting smaller and smaller below him. He felt wonderful! It was just as good as he had known it would be. As he gained in confidence, he swooped and he swerved. He was born to fly and everyone could see it now.

Now Puggle was an extraordinary pig, but he was a pig all the same. He found himself steering towards his home.

Puggle looked down at the farm. It seemed very, very far away. His pigsty was a tiny dot in the corner of the farmyard. His feed trough was an even tinier dot. Puggle felt a pang. It hit him somewhere between his ribs in a place that he liked to keep full of something tasty. It occurred to him that several hours had passed since breakfast. Exciting hours. Amazing hours. But hours completely lacking in any kind of pig-pleasing nourishment.

Puggle throttled back and prepared to land. In the great celestial struggle between flying and eating, there's really no contest...

The Best Birthday Cake

Amanda Sarah Jane Jones was looking forward to her birthday party. She had invited everyone in her class at school and given her parents strict instructions about the food, the music, the balloons and the party bags they should arrange. Her mother and father, seeing a very determined glint in her eye and her foot poised to stamp, had hastily agreed to all her ideas. It was, after all, her birthday. It was also six months away, but Amanda Sarah Jane was the kind of girl who believed in starting her campaigns early.

In the months that followed her demands, Amanda went to the birthday parties of several of her friends. If they had giant balloons, she soon told her long-suffering parents she needed super-giant balloons. If they had two tasty kinds of sandwiches, she ordered three kinds. Her party would be better than anyone's.

But as the weeks passed, and she went to even more parties, Amanda began to see that her plans had a big hole in them, and it was a hole right in the middle where a birthday cake should be. Polly, who had her own pony, had a special cake in the shape of her beloved Velvet. Akiko's father made her a cake shaped like an enormous kite, with liquorice strings and candy bows. Xavier, whose birthday was near Hallowe'en, had a cake shaped like a pumpkin – and it was hollow and had a candle inside.

Amanda became very thoughtful.

About a month before her birthday, she tried to make her parents understand the importance of this feature of her party.

"You see," she said, "the cake is the centre of everything. It has to be carried in near the end so that everyone can sing Happy Birthday to me and be amazed."

"Be amazed?" asked her father. "By what exactly?"

"By the cake!" said Amanda. This was going to be harder than she thought.

"Are people amazed by cakes?" asked her mother. "I don't think I've ever been amazed by a cake. Have you, Pete?"

"I've been amazed by rock cakes," said her husband with some feeling. "I cracked a tooth on your mother's."

"My mother is an excellent cook!" Amanda's mother sounded frosty. "She taught me everything I know."

There was an unpleasant silence as both Amanda and her father tried to think of something tactful to say. But Mrs. Jones was going on.

"I was thinking of one of my big chocolate cakes, but with candles on top," she said. "That would be okay, wouldn't it?"

Amanda's father exchanged a glance with his daughter. "I guess it wouldn't be *amazing*," he said. "Maybe we should buy one this time. They do them for all the popular TV characters now, you know."

"Well!" cried Mrs. Jones.

"No!" cried Amanda.

"There," said her mother, "I knew my chocolate cake would be fine."

"No!" Amanda felt the moment had come to be firm. "I don't want a chocolate cake and I don't want a bought cake. I want a special cake that no one else has ever had. And I want it to be huge. I was thinking that a Princess's Palace would be good, with flags from the turrets, lights at the windows and music coming out of it."

"Flags?"

"Lights?"

"Music?"

Amanda's parents looked bemused.

"You could order it from that shop in the Mall," Amanda explained, making her voice patient and friendly as if she was talking to two-year-olds.

"We'll see," said her mother. "It's not a bad idea. I'll be very busy with the other food. It would be good to have the cake taken out of my hands."

On Saturday, the whole family went shopping, and Amanda made sure they "happened" to pass the cake shop she had in mind.

"Oh look," she said brightly. "We might as well go and see about my cake since we're here." And in they went.

The shop assistant began by talking to Amanda's parents, but it soon became clear who was in charge, so she and Amanda had a long discussion about the details of the cake, and the assistant really entered into the spirit of the thing.

"How about fluorescent icing?" she said, "so that you could turn the lights out when the cake was brought in? And we could make smoke come out of the base, like mist, you know, to add to the air of fairytale magic."

Amanda agreed to the fluorescent icing but turned down the mist on the grounds that it might get out of hand and hide the wonderful cake. Eventually, she and the assistant had everything settled between them.

"I'll send an estimate of the price to you, shall I?" she asked Amanda's parents. "It's only a formality, but it helps to sort these things out in advance."

"That's a good idea," said Mr. Jones.

A week passed, and Amanda spent quite a lot of it telling her friends at school about the amazing birthday cake she had ordered. She didn't give any details because she wanted it to be a surprise, but she dropped hints about hugeness and special effects that made her friends turn emerald with envy.

But on Saturday morning, as the family sat down to breakfast, Amanda's father began to open the mail. All of a sudden, he turned pale and clutched his chest with a strangled gasp.

"Pete, what is it? Amanda, call an ambulance!" cried her mother, but Mr .Jones waved a feeble hand to stop her.

"It's th-th-the estimate f-f-from the c-c-cake shop," he stuttered. "Look!"

Mrs Jones looked ... and had to sit down. "It must be a joke," she said and hurried to the telephone.

Five minutes later, it was clear that the extraordinarily enormous amount of money in the estimate was not a joke.

"I will *not* remortgage the house!" cried Mr. Jones dramatically.

Mrs. Jones was even more heroic. "You just tell me exactly what you want, darling," she told her daughter, "and I'll make it for you, even if I have to work night and day."

Amanda felt doubtful. She looked doubtful, too. But she could see there was very little choice. She began to outline her cherished plans.

A week before the party, Mrs. Jones rolled up her sleeves and started work.

"Would you like me to help?" asked her husband, putting his head around the kitchen door.

"No!" cried Mrs. Jones, thinking of a truly disastrous egg-boiling incident.

"No!" cried Amanda, thinking of the exploding sardines episode.

As Mr. Jones slunk away, Amanda and her mother began mixing truly huge quantities of ingredients. Every pan and bowl in the kitchen was called into service. The cooker only just took the strain, as batch after batch of mixture was cooked. Several layers of the cake were carried next door for Mrs. Mason to cook. Pretty soon the whole kitchen was filled with cooling cakes, while an exhausted Mrs. Jones flopped against the sink.

"Tomorrow," she said, "we'll get started on assembling it. Don't, whatever you do, let the dog into the kitchen!" For she could hear Ruffles whining at the door, his nose tickled by the tasty smell of cakes – dozens of them – cooking and cooling only a few feet away.

Early next morning the whole family began the task of putting the cake together. This time Mr. Jones was allowed to help, for he claimed to  have engineering experience. Mrs. Jones privately suspected that this consisted of mending his bike when he was six, but she said nothing.

Mr. Jones' first contribution was an enormous board to place on the kitchen table, for the cake was much too big for any plate in the house. Mrs. Jones covered the board with foil and Amanda went round afterwards smoothing it out, even the parts that wouldn't be seen. She wanted everything to be perfect, after all. Then the building could begin.

It took all day to place one piece of cake on top of another. The parts were glued together with strawberry jam, and some were cut out to resemble towers, battlements and a grand staircase at the front. Amanda was the architect. Mrs. Jones did the precise cutting. Mr. Jones stood on a stepladder to position the turrets at the very top.

When the whole thing was finished, the Jones family stood back to admire it.

"That turret isn't straight," said the architect critically. "And the steps are wonky, too."

"It will settle overnight," said Mr. Jones airily. "And the icing will cover up a multitude of sins ... I mean, the icing will transform it completely."

Once again, Ruffles was banished to the hall and the doors were firmly shut. The cake was left in the darkness.

It was an early start again for the Jones family next day. Gallons and gallons of icing had to be mixed. Mr. Jones brightly suggested using the washing machine, but his wife's expression warned him not to pursue the matter.

The plan was for the icing to be the palest, prettiest pink, but the stuff that colours icing is very, very strong. Mr. Jones, measuring it out with a tablespoon instead of a teaspoon, managed to create a bowl of the brightest magenta icing you have ever seen. It looked revolting.

"I think white would be much more elegant," said Amanda firmly, hiding the bottle of pink stuff under the sink. She couldn't bear any more accidents to her wonderful cake.

Icing the cake was the trickiest part so far. Mrs. Jones tried spreading it very, very gently with a knife. Amanda tried dribbling it on with a spoon. Mr. Jones experimented with a throw-it-at-the-cake-and-see-if-it-sticks technique, which nearly demolished the north turret. Amanda had to confiscate his bowl of icing and instruct him on making little silver flags instead.

By the middle of the afternoon, with the cake only half iced, conditions in the kitchen became unbearable. It was partly because Mr. Jones was sulking over his flag-making. It was partly because Mrs. Jones was getting back-ache trying to reach the top of the cake. It was partly because Amanda kept checking on both her parents. But it was mostly because Ruffles would not stop whining outside the door. Even an extra-large bowl of doggy chunks didn't subdue him. The shut door made him absolutely sure that the family was having a good time without him, and he wasn't happy about it.

Mrs Jones turned on the radio to drown out the sounds. Ruffles stopped whining and started howling. The family found whining was better, but Mr. Jones was so desperate he stuffed a couple of bits of cake into his ears to try to shut it out. Don't try this at home. It doesn't work and it means you have crumbs on your collars for weeks afterwards.

It was almost midnight when the icing was finished at last. Amanda and her parents staggered up to bed, praying they never saw another cake as long as they lived. And Ruffles, still shut out of the kitchen, chewed the stair carpet in disgust.

The next morning, although all of them felt rather queasy at the sight of the cake, the Jones family began the final decorations. The party was at two o'clock, so everything had to be ready by then. Amanda positioned the flags (her Dad had to hold her up) and painted windows and doors with the famous fluorescent icing.

Mrs. Jones carefully put candles all around the base. Mr. Jones was in charge of the electronics. There were fairy lights to fix and the tiny radio to slide into a special hole in the side to play princess music when the big moment came.

At last everything was completely ready. Amanda stepped back and looked at her cake. There had been times over the last few days when she had wished she had never thought of it, but now she saw that it had all been worth it.

"Now keep all the doors shut," said Mrs Jones, as she rushed about, getting all the other elements of the party ready. "We don't want a disaster with Ruffles at the last moment." Ruffles made his feelings known in the usual way.

By half past one, Amanda was in her party dress and blowing up the last balloon. She had butterflies in her stomach and almost everywhere else. She had never felt so nervous. Even her parents entering races at Sports Day wasn't as worrying as this.

At seven minutes past two exactly, the first guests began to arrive. Ruffles, as a special treat, was allowed to join in the fun. The party got underway. Everything was just as wonderful as Amanda had planned. And the main attraction was yet to come.

By five o'clock, it was already dark. In the kitchen, Mr. and Mrs. Jones peered at the list of instructions their daughter had given them. Slowly, the hands of the clock clicked into place. It was time to carry in the cake!

"On my count," said Mr. Jones. "One, two, three, lift!" He was glad he had called in the neighbours to help. Two people could never have lifted the monster cake. The Masons and the Jones shuffled towards the door, the cake swaying between them. But two feet from the door a huge problem became clear. Width of cake: four feet five inches. Width of door: two feet ten inches. Result: disaster!

"Wait! Wait!" cried Mr. Jones. "Let me think!"

"Be quick!" cried Mrs. Jones. "I can't hold this for much longer!"

"The french windows! We can carry it around the outside of the house!" gasped her husband.

Mrs. Jones looked at him in frank astonishment. Yes, it would work! It was a good idea! "Everyone take four paces to the left!" she called.

Swaying dangerously, the cake was edged through the large kitchen window. It was not an easy task, but the team was not going to be beaten now. The Masons balanced the cake on the window sill as the Jones rushed around through the back door to take up the other side.

Then the cake was on the move again, slowly tottering down the path at the side of the house and round to the french windows in the party room.

"Can we come in?" called Mr. Jones. It was a signal. When Amanda heard the call, she was to turn off the lights so that the cake could make its grand entrance. At the same time, Mr. Jones nudged the switch on the battery (he had positioned it so he could reach it with his nose!) to turn on the fairy lights and the music. Mr. Mason, very cleverly, managed to open the doors with his bottom.

"Happy birthday to you!
Happy birthday to you…"

As the singing began and the doors swung open, a terrifying noise came from the party room.

"*Yaaaaaaarrrrooooooow!*" Ruffles, seeing the cake he had been so tantalized by all week, leapt forward with a howl of joy. Mr. Mason, seeing something furry with gleaming eyes flying towards him in the dark, crumpled to his knees with a cry of terror. The cake, jiggling like something alive, slid with a terrible inevitability onto the carpet —upside down.

Amanda turned on the lights when she heard the sickening thud. A mountain of cake and jam and icing filled the centre of the room. The fairy lights had been buried, but they somehow gave an eerie glow to the whole mess. Somewhere deep inside the cake, the radio was playing the Dance of the Sugar Plum Fairy.

Mr. Jones took one look at the musical Matterhorn and fled into the garden, falling over the fence in his hurry.

Amanda opened her mouth to cry and found something very much like a laugh coming out. After all that work. After all that planning. After all that...

The party guests stood like statues with their mouths open. They had been to pirate parties and fairy parties and cowboy parties. Never in their wildest dreams had they thought of holding a flying-cake party!

Mrs. Jones, worn out with days of work on the cake, could think only of the radio. Was strawberry jam even now glooping into its inner workings? She lost her head completely.

"A special prize to the first one to find the radio!" she cried, and twenty gleeful children and one excited dog leaped forward, howling with delight.

What else is there to say? The radio was found—eventually. The room was cleaned—eventually. Nineteen very happy and very sticky children went home, and one happy and very sticky child went up to bed with a blissful smile on her face.

"Thanks, Mum. Thanks, Dad," she said sleepily. "It wasn't what I planned but it was a party everyone will talk about for ever. And the cake was really, *really* ... amazing!"

The Talkative Tree

Far away and long ago, a talkative tree caused incredible trouble. This is how it happened.

Not everyone realizes that trees talk, although you have probably heard them do it. The language is made up of rustles and creaks, swooshes and swishes. It is a language that only other trees understand. Of course, as young trees they can only understand trees from the same area. It takes a long time for an oak tree, say, to learn how to talk to a Japanese cherry, and some trees are too snooty to try to get on with their neighbours.

That wasn't the problem with the tree in this story. He was very friendly. Igthorp, as he was called, grew up as a young sapling in the middle of a big forest on a hill. All around him were trees of every kind. He loved to chat to the holly on his left and the maple on his right.

In fact, Igthorp liked to chat a little too much. No, the truth must be told. He liked to chat a lot too much. All day and all night he prattled away, and the other trees longed for a little peace and quiet.

It wasn't as if Igthorp said anything interesting. He simply came out with the first thing that came into his head. And he wasn't a very clever tree either, so what he had to say wasn't earth-shattering in any way. He talked about the weather—a lot. He wondered about what the sky was made of—a lot. He complained that worms were tickling his roots—a lot. He talked about his childhood, his bark trouble (don't ask—it was some kind of disease) and his awkward branch that was making him lean slightly forward.

Now, compared with you and me, trees are patient creatures. They can set about doing something and not mind if it takes a hundred years. The trees around Igthorp voted with their roots. Day by day, they edged a fraction of an inch away from their noisy neighbour.

Igthorp was too busy talking to notice it happening. After all, he never stopped for a moment to hear what anyone else said. But all the same, he felt a bit lonely the day he discovered he was totally alone. What happened was that a rabbit, eager to make a new home for her little ones, began digging among his roots.

That made Igthorp pause for a moment in what he was saying (and had been saying for the last seventy years) and look down. As he did so, he noticed for the very first time that he was standing on the top of a hill, completely alone. Down in the valley, on every side, there were trees as far as the eye could see. But he was alone. All the other trees had shuffled off and left him.

From far, far away he could hear a tantalizing whispering, as the other trees chatted to each other. But they were much too far to hear. Igthorp wiggled his roots to discourage the rabbit and started to talk. It was the only thing he knew how to do, and the fact that there was no one to hear him didn't change the fact that he had things to say.

"Ho hum," said Igthorp. "It looks like rain. Hmm. It looked like rain the day before yesterday, too. Hmm. I wonder if it will rain tomorrow. I wonder if it will really rain today. Hmm. That rabbit has gone. Good. Hmm. And my bark isn't quite so itchy today. Hmm. It was pretty itchy yesterday. It might be itchy again tomorrow. Hmm. That sky is getting greyer. It might be snow, not rain. Snow. That's a nice word. Sno-o-o-w. It's soft, like snow. Sno-o-o-w. Hmm. No, I think

I was wrong. It is going to be rain. Sno-o-o-ow. It's a nice word. Sno-o-o-w. But I think it will be rain. Hmm. I'm glad that rabbit's gone. Hmm. I'm glad my bark isn't itchy today. Hmm. Yes, I think it is going to rain. Today. Hmm."

You'll understand now why an entire forest, subjected to twenty-four hours of this every day, shuffled down the hill. Igthorp, however, was blissfully unaware that he was impossible to live with. He had never stopped talking long enough for somebody to be able to tell him. As the clouds grew darker and darker, he muttered on.

Igthorp was right. It did rain. It poured down, drenching the tree and

everything around. The rabbit, out on the open hillside, scurried back among the big tree's roots, and Igthorp didn't have the heart to wiggle her out again.

The rain lashed down on Igthorp's leaves. The sky grew darker and darker. Almost overhead, a mighty roll of thunder drummed among the dark grey clouds. Then, suddenly, a flash of lightning streaked across the sky, looking for somewhere to strike. And what was the highest thing for miles around? It was Igthorp, still muttering to himself about the rain.

Strr-i-i-i-i-ke! The lightning sizzled on to Igthorp's topmost branches. For a moment he stood there, lit up and glowing. Then little tongues of flame licked among his leaves, leaving him looking blackened and dead.

There was a dreadful silence on top of the hill … until a very familiar voice struck up once more…

"Well, well, what was that? I've been sizzled! I've been struck! I knew it would rain. But I didn't know there would be lightning, too. How exciting! Sizzled and struck! Hmm. I wonder if it will rain tomorrow? I wonder if it will thunder tomorrow? I wonder if the lightning will come? They say lightning never strikes twice in the same place, but you never know. I might be lucky again. Hmm.

What's that wiggling? Oh, that rabbit again. Her ears look a bit singed. Serves her right. Hmm. It might be sunny in a minute. Is that a rainbow? I like rainbows. I wonder if it will rain tomorrow."

To anyone looking at him, Igthorp seemed a pitiful wreck. His leaves were dead. His branches were blackened and broken. His trunk was dark and charred. But inside, Igthorp felt just the same. He was ready for another seventy years of standing on the hill.

But Igthorp didn't have even seventy days there. At the end of the week, a tractor chugged up the tree with two men on board. They jumped off and took a long look at the tree.

"This one's dead," said the first man. "But it's pretty old. The wood should be fine inside."

They didn't even bother to chop Igthorp down. They looped a chain around his trunk and attached it to the back of the tractor. Then they drove off down the hill.

Igthorp felt a heaving in his roots. He heard a great screeching sound and began to topple towards the ground. With his mighty roots wiggling up into the air, it was difficult to tell which way up he was. A rather alarmed rabbit jumped down from the roots and hopped safely to the ground. She had noticed that the hole left by Igthorp might make the beginnings of a very fine home indeed.

Igthorp was dragged down the hill and along a rough track. And all the time he was talking. Of course, the men on the tractor just heard branches scraping on the ground and twigs breaking, but what Igthorp was really saying went something like this…

"Well, well, pulled up by my roots, well, well. Hmm. I wonder where they're taking me? I didn't realize my roots were so big. Where's that rabbit now? I can't go carrying rabbits around. Hmm. It doesn't seem to be here. That's good. Hmm. I wonder if it will rain tomorrow. Hmm. I wonder where we're going? I wonder if it's far? I wonder if we'll get there before the rain comes?"

It wasn't long before Igthorp found out. At the end of the track was a large building from which came a terrible noise. It was the sawmill. Happily chattering away, Igthorp was dragged towards the whizzing blades.

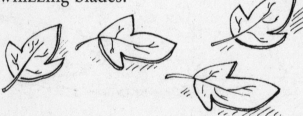

From that day, there was silence on top of the hill, broken only by the squeaking of tens, then hundreds, then thousands of baby rabbits, who popped up year after year. With so many wriggling, squiggling babies around, no more trees grew on top of the hill, and the whispering of the forest in the valley seemed very far away.

Meanwhile, the years passed and nothing was heard of old Igthorp. But a President had to be dragged from his office. "The table just wouldn't stop talking!" he cried, as the men in white coats took him away.

And a boy in Denmark refused to take his coat off because, he said, his chair told him it was going to rain.

This morning, I put my creaky old table out into the garden. I have bought a new one that looks much, much better. But, you know, it's a very strange thing. I'm sure that the hedge used to be nearer the house. And the tree by the pond no longer has its toes in the water. I expect I'm imagining it, don't you?

The Supersonic Sandwich

Some people are happy to play games and enter competitions just for the fun of it. "It's the taking part that counts," they cry, merrily shaking the hand of the winner. When tempers are frayed over the snakes and ladders board or sharp words are spoken on the tennis court, they beam and cry, "It's only a game!" To the kind of people who take games *seriously*, these puny players are intensely annoying.

Mrs. Brangs was a woman who took games seriously. She clenched her teeth in fury when her husband beat her at *Snap!*

She went purple with rage when Mrs. Wootten cheated at croquet. When Dora Devereaux's dog upset the Monopoly board in the middle of a tense battle between Mayfair and Marlborough Street, Mrs. Brangs almost lost the power of speech. She was a woman who liked to win—and to win by a wide margin.

Well, we've all met people like that. You may be one yourself. It may drive you wild when your friends giggle instead of concentrating during a dominoes duel. Perhaps you're the type who trains at dawn for sports day races and doesn't even consider the concept of second place. The difference with Mrs. Brangs (and I know you are not this kind of person, for you wouldn't have time to read this book if you were) was that she had a memory like an elephant. She remembered every point she lost to an opponent. She could recall the tiniest waiving of the rules and the slightest short-sightedness on the part of a referee. Stored up in her fevered brain was every game she had ever played and the conduct of her fellow players. She respected very few of them.

It is strange, really, that the people of Little Bassington didn't realize what seething emotions boiled beneath Mrs. Brangs' less-than-calm exterior. But then they were the relaxed kind of people I mentioned at the beginning. As they didn't take such things seriously themselves, it never entered their heads that an avenging angel lived in their midst. They thought dear Hilda was short on temper and long on determination, that was all.

But at 19, Alba Crescent, Mrs. Brangs was plotting her revenge. She wanted once and for all to show up her neighbours as the lily-livered, feeble-minded, shilly-shallying bunch of no-hopers she believed them to be. And fate played right into her hands.

One spring morning, young Doris Devereaux (and her dog) bounced into the village shop, where most of the older ladies of the village were buying their

weekly groceries and Mrs. Hilda Brangs was taking a peek at the answers in the back of last week's *Puzzler's Paradise* magazine to see if she had won anything.

"Oh, ladies!" gushed Doris. "It's *sooo* exciting!"

"What is?" asked several ladies, at once giving Doris the audience she was longing for. Mrs. Brangs sighed. She felt sure that nothing the silly woman could have to say could possibly be of interest to her. But she was wrong.

"The judges are coming!" cried Doris, her voice rising almost to a shriek in her excitement. "They're coming *here*! They're coming *next week*! It's too, too exciting for words!"

"Apparently not," muttered Mrs. Brangs under her breath, but even she had been interested by the mention of judges. It sounded as though some kind of deadly competition was afoot, and as we know, there is nothing Mrs. Brangs likes better than a contest of some description.

It took half an hour and two cups of tea for Doris to get her news out at last. It turned out that the judges of the *Biggest Ever Book of Records* were coming to the village to film a huge television spectacular. And whenever they did that, they liked local people to try to break some records.

Mrs. Brangs' brain was working overtime, but she spoke quite casually to the ladies in the shop.

"It'll mean bell-ringing," she said darkly, "for hours and hours and hours. I dread to think how long the world record is. It could be *weeks*!"

"No," said Doris triumphantly. "It won't be that. I can tell you definitely that it won't be that."

"How do you know? What else do you know? Has the list of competitions been published already?" Mrs. Brangs was desperate to know.

But Doris just giggled in a silly way. "There are workmen on the church tower," she said. "They won't be able to ring the bells for months."

Of course! Mrs. Brangs was furious with herself. She had known that all along and now she felt that she had revealed to the others just how interested she was in the whole project. Strolling as casually as she could (which frankly deceived nobody), she left the shop and dashed home. It was all she could do not to break into a run as she neared her gate.

As soon as she was indoors, Mrs. Brangs tore off her coat and hurried to the telephone. Her fingers literally shook as she dialled her nephew's number.

"Felix?" she cried, as soon as the ringing was answered. "Is that you?"

"Yes, of course," said a cross voice, similar in many ways to Mrs. Brangs' own.

"What do you want, Aunty?"

Mrs. Brangs explained at once. "I need you to look something up on your computer," she said. "It's about the *Biggest Ever Book of Records* coming to Little Bassington. I need to know what the competitions are going to be. Isn't there a spidersite or something you can check out? I need to know all there is to know about this, and I need to know by first thing tomorrow morning at the latest."

Felix hesitated. He felt that he was in a strong position for negotiating his next birthday present, and he was right. Two computer games and four CDs later, he had come to an agreement with his aunt.

Mrs. Brangs hardly slept. It was so hard to plan when she had no idea what the competitions would be. Next morning she was waiting inside the front door for the postman, almost gnawing the door

mat, when she heard his footsteps on the path. As the letters appeared, she seized them so forcefully that the postman felt in danger of losing his hand.

Back at her breakfast table, Mrs. Brangs discarded several bills and a brochure about stair-carpets and tore open Felix's envelope.

"Dear Aunty," she read, "here is the list you were looking for. I wouldn't attempt the trampolining if I were you."

Mrs. Brangs skimmed the list so quickly she couldn't take it in. Then she read more slowly, considering each item.

1. Shrimp-shelling: the number of shrimps that can be shelled in twelve minutes.
2. Trampolining: the number of back somersaults achieved in four minutes.
3. Pie-throwing: the number of pies to reach the target (details enclosed) in two minutes.
4. Leapfrog: largest team for a continuous game of leapfrog. Number to beat: 2,986.
5. Orange-juggling: highest number of oranges that can be kept in the air in continuous motion for a period of seven minutes (see rules for size and weight of oranges – no fruit substitutions allowed).
6. Marathon singing: longest period of non-stop singing. No repetitions (see rules for break times, decibel levels and measures of tunefulness).

7. Sandwich-making: highest
sandwich in two minutes using
standard bread and no two fillings
the same (see rules for buttering and
depth of filling allowed in each layer).
8. Ear-waggling: biggest range of
movement and longest sustained
waggling (no wiggling permitted)
using measures supplied.

For one mad moment, Mrs.
Brangs saw herself and the whole village
of Little Bassington leapfrogging madly
across the green. Then she pulled herself
together. There simply weren't 2,986 able-
bodied people in Little Bassington and she
didn't fancy the idea of leapfrogging with
strangers. Mrs. Brangs turned back to the
list to give it more serious consideration.

Shrimp-shelling? It wasn't a pleasant
thought. Mrs. Brangs had never enjoyed
seafood and as a result she had very little
experience of shelling shrimps. (It was

hard enough to say, never mind do.)
Besides, old Mrs. Moleworthy was a
fishmonger's daughter and had been
raised to do all kinds of barely speakable
things to fish. She was sure to win. Mrs.
Brangs discarded the shrimp-shelling with
some relief.

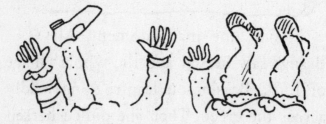

Trampolining? To be frank, Felix
might have a point in warning her away
from this one. Mrs. Brangs still felt full of
vim and vigour, but even she would have
to confess that she was not in her first
youth. Even with training, she was
unlikely to triumph over the slim girls
from the village school. No, trampolining
was out.

Pie-throwing was next on the list, and here Mrs. Brangs felt more confident. She had a powerful right arm and her left was not weak either. She imagined—oh, how vividly—throwing pies at the faces of all her enemies in Little Bassington (a large figure, though not as large as 2,986). But a quick look at the rules revealed that the target was to be a cardboard one, hung frighteningly high from a kind of scaffold. Some of the excitement of the event seemed to evaporate for Mrs. Brangs. She remembered, too, that the local police-man, Officer Pingling, had an even stronger right arm than her own. Would he feel it beneath his dignity to compete? If his recent pin-the-tail-on-the-donkey performance was anything to go by, almost certainly not. Mrs. Brangs still smarted from his scathing comments on her tail-positioning, during which he had given her more detail about a donkey's anatomy than she had felt was entirely essential. Maybe pie-throwing wasn't such a good idea.

The next two were easily disposed of. Leapfrogging was out of the question and juggling had never been Mrs. Brangs' favourite pastime. She could manage a fairly respectable three-orange performance, but anything more was beyond her, and she only had a week to practise. No, not orange-juggling.

Marathon singing? Now, that was more like it. Mrs. Brangs, it will not, I'm sure, surprise you to learn, possessed a powerful vocal instrument. In church on Sundays she belted out the hymns with no thought for the ear-drums of the members of the congregation in front of her. But was endurance really her greatest skill? To be truthful, Mrs. Brangs was stronger on volume than she was on the long haul.

And that bit about tunefulness in the rules could pose a challenge. Although Mrs. Brangs was personally quite confident of her pitch, she had overheard one or two comments that made her doubt the hearing of some listeners. Who could say what the judges would feel about her intonation? Mrs. Brangs mentally put marathon singing to one side. It was a possibility if nothing else appealed.

Running her eyes down the list, Mrs. Brangs saw that she had only two more to choose from – and one of those was ear-waggling. She knew that she need waste no time over that particular skill. She didn't have it, and that was that.

Only one more contest remained. Sandwich-making. As she read the rules in some detail, Mrs. Brang felt her interest rising. Surely this was absolutely the kind of thing at which she could excel? It called for speed and determination. Fine. It required planning and inventiveness. Also fine. And it was sure to involve a head-to-head, no-holds-barred play-off against Dora Devereaux, who prided herself on her culinary skills. Better than fine. This was truly *excellent*! Mrs. Brangs rubbed her hands and set about making her own list. Already, a sandwich of truly gigantic proportions was growing in her mind. Dora Devereaux didn't stand a chance.

Mrs. Brangs made her preparations with care. She had practice sessions in her own kitchen until her husband prayed he would never see another sandwich. She added and added and added to her list of fillings, discarding those that were fiddly or unreliable from a stackability point of view. She thought carefully about how she would set out her containers of fillings and buckets of butter. She even practised climbing up and down stepladders at speed—she was very confident, as you can see, that her own sandwich would tower over whatever the competition could do.

On the day of the contest itself, Mrs. Brangs was up well before the break of dawn, ready to make her final preparations.

Absolutely key to these was getting the butter to just the right degree of softness, so that it would spread easily but not fall off her knife. Mr. Brangs  was given the task of testing but his wife still hovered over him. A mistake at this stage could be critical.

At two o'clock, the village green was throbbing with people. The television crew had erected platforms from which the contests could be viewed. Areas were taped off so that the spectators could be kept at a distance. At ten past two precisely, the shrimp-shelling got off to a shaky start when Mrs. Moleworthy had one of her turns and had to sit down. Mr. Prentice, her chief opponent, objected that this gave her an unfair advantage. A

close and lengthy scrutiny of the rules revealed that competitors could shell shrimps on their heads if they wanted, and the contest got underway at last thirty-three minutes late. It was close, but Mrs. Moleworthy won by three shrimps, although she did not break the record in the *Biggest Ever Book of Records.*

The trampolining went off without a hitch, although one camera-man got too enthusiastic and was thumped in the ear by a bouncing elbow. The girls did well, but again, no world records were broken.

It was a different story in the pie-throwing, and Mrs. Brangs shuddered at how close she had come to almost total humiliation. Not only was Officer Pingling frighteningly good, but Mrs. Mabble from the school showed surprising form. It was later revealed that she had been national shot-put champion before her marriage but tended to keep it quiet because her husband thought it unladylike.

Mrs. Mabble walked off with the honours and a new world record. And Officer Pingling, dripping with sweat, stumbled home to the derisive cheers of several small boys who had met with his disapproval in the past.

The leapfrog, as Mrs. Brangs had suspected, was rather a disappointment.

Most of the leapers were very much less than froglike. The event ended in an ungainly heap with Mrs. Brang's husband somewhere at the bottom of it. But the director rubbed his hands with glee and said that it made good television.

Ear-waggling, it seemed, did not make good television. Apart from the fact that there was only one contestant (young Jimmy Barnes having been disqualified on the discovery of a contraption made of string and chewing gum attached to his left lobe), the waggling was so minor that the director shook his head. Mr. Devereaux (Dora's husband's ancient father) was given a consolation prize and hurried off the stage.

By now, it was late afternoon. Things were not running to schedule and a note of desperation had entered the director's voice. The light was fading. The camera-men were fading. And many of the spectators were fading, too. It was decided to hold the orange-juggling and the sandwich-making at the same time.

Mrs. Brangs, of course, protested. She objected that it would be off-putting to see oranges flying about out of the corner of her eye, but she had no support from Dora Devereaux, who was always anxious to please. As a result, Mrs. Brangs was over-ruled and the contestants were told to prepare for the whistle.

Ready! Set! Wheeeeeeeeeeeeeee! The ladies roared into action. Bread was slapped on to tables. Butter flew from glinting knives. The first fillings splodged into place. After the first thirty seconds of panic, Mrs. Brangs hit her stride. She whistled through ham, corned beef, tuna and tomato, cucumber, pastrami, chicken mayonnaise and chopped egg with capers.

The sandwich was already up to her eyebrows, so she called for the stepladder and plunged on, knowing that she could not spare the time to look over her shoulder at what Dora Devereaux was doing behind her.

Avocado, jelly, bacon, salad, peanut butter, banana,

cheese, chocolate and honey followed rapidly. Mrs. Brangs steadied her tottering pile with a firm hand.

"Just one minute left!" called the official referee, and Mrs. Brangs got her second wind. Liver, duck, beef, lamb, aubergine, peas, pork, oyster, shrimp (despite her feelings about seafood), cod, salmon, trout, onion, turkey, sausage, marmalade and marshmallow were hurled between slices. Mrs. Brangs was getting to the end of her containers of fillings. Only the stranger ones were left. Ostrich, ice cream, kangaroo, cauliflower, squid and mango were slapped into place. Panting,

Mrs. Brangs glanced at the clock. Four seconds to go and no more fillings! In the heat of the competition she had been faster than she had ever managed in practice.

Three and a half seconds to go and Mrs. Brangs made the mistake of looking over her left shoulder. There was Dora Devereaux, wobbling dangerously at the very top of her stepladder and just about to place pilchards and peppers on the very top of her extraordinary sandwich. Mrs. Brangs tried to estimate the height of the two piles. It was impossible. But it was close. It was much, much too close for comfort.

Mrs. Brangs was bursting with the need to win. Just at that moment an orange shot up near her left ear. She had totally forgotten about the other contest, still going on right next door. In a moment of madness, Mrs. Brangs, beside herself with anxiety, stretched out her hand and caught an orange. She threw herself down the ladder, scarcely touching a step. *Chop, chop, chop! Slap, slip, slop!* Mrs. Brangs made short work of the orange and buttered another slice. Then she hurtled up the steps again, purple in the face, and plonked it on to the top of her pile, *just* as the final whistle sounded.

Neither Mrs. Brangs (who was now an unbecoming shade of puce) nor Dora Devereaux (collapsed under her table) heard much of the judging that followed.

Tape measures were produced, careful judgements as to depths of fillings were discussed, and each layer was examined minutely for traces of non-edible fillings or failure to butter. It seemed endless. By the time it was over, both ladies were fully recovered and gnawing their nails.

The announcer spoke to camera. "And what an exciting finish this has been. Once again *The Biggest Ever Book of Records* has brought you excitement and drama. And I can tell you now that the world record *has* been broken (wild cheers from the crowd) and that the effort of both ladies was truly outstanding (even wilder cheers from the crowd, a smile from Dora Devereaux and a weak wave from Mrs. Hilda Brangs)."

There was a dramatic pause. Then the announcer gave a wink and went on, "The highest sandwich, a quite staggering fifteen centimetres higher than the world record, was that of Mrs. Hilda Brangs! Congratulations, Mrs. Brangs!"

Mrs. Brangs' large bosom filled with pride. She was a champion. A world champion! And Dora Devereaux—*hah!*—was nowhere. Mrs. Brangs couldn't resist turning to look at her opponent, and what she saw sent a chill down her spine. There was Dora, standing next to the announcer. And Dora *had a sinister smile on her face.*

With a sickening certainty, Mrs. Brangs knew what the announcer was going to say before the wretched man opened his mouth.

"But there was, as I said, drama right up to the last moment. Sadly, Mrs. Brangs has been disqualified—*for deliberately disrupting another contest*! Let's see that replay now!"

Mrs. Brangs didn't need to see in slow motion the moment when her hand stretched out and caught the orange. She didn't need to see the pitiful face of the juggler as his hand closed around thin air and he dropped the lot as a result. Instead, she silently and stealthily crept away, vowing never to compete again ... but to devote all her energies to the dark and dreadful downfall of Dora Devereaux.

Mrs. Wolf's Problem

Mrs. Wolf had a problem and it can be stated right away. She had a son called William who was neither big nor bad. That, for a storybook wolf, is a truly terrible disgrace. Any wolf worth his or her salt has a long history of eating little pigs (preferably three at a time) and old ladies (especially when they're ill in bed). They are also supposed to frighten little girls, lurk about in the dark near flocks of sheep, and howl convincingly whenever there is a moonlit night.

William did none of these things. At first his mother thought that it was simply because he was a rather small cub and he would grow out of it. But even when he was fully grown, he only came up to her shoulder. His teeth, although sharp and white, were not big enough to inspire terror in most sensible people. His eyes, although bright and cunning, did not glint in a menacing way. He didn't drool. He didn't lurk. And his howl was rather tuneful and not at all heart-stopping.

Mrs. Wolf was in despair. First of all she tried sending him for lessons to old Septimus Wolf in the Deep Dark Forest. Septimus had a truly nasty reputation. A reputation that any wolf would be proud of. It was said that his lair was decorated with the bones of his victims. Others said that wasn't true. Septimus had eaten them, bones and all.

It was a rather cautious William who poked his snout into the old wolf's lair for his first lesson in viciousness.

Septimus, however, was asleep in front of a cosy fire. William expected him to leap up and start snarling at any moment, but instead a gentle snoring came from his slobbery lips. It was warm and comfortable by the fire, so after a while, William too lay down and went to sleep with his head on his paws.

When William woke up several hours later, it was already getting dark and time to go home again. Septimus, too, stirred and yawned.

"You must be young William," he mumbled. "Is it time for your lesson?"

William shook his head.

"No, it's time I was going home again. Shall I come back tomorrow?"

"That's a good idea," said Septimus, thinking of the generous fee he was going to receive from William's mother. "Little and often is the best way of learning."

That night, Mrs. Wolf questioned her son on what he had learnt that day.

"Was there any discussion of the importance of pouncing?" she asked. "Did you practise whining and scrabbling? Show me what you did."

William paused. "I don't think I should," he said truthfully. He knew that his mother was expecting great things of him and of old Septimus.

Mrs. Wolf nodded wisely. "Least said, soonest mended," she said. "I think I understand. I don't blame Septimus for swearing you to secrecy. A wolf's most vicious techniques are something he treasures. Come and have your supper. I'm sure you've deserved it."

For three weeks, William spent every day asleep in front of the fire with Septimus. It made him rather wakeful at night, so that he took to sloping off into the dark and sniffing around the sheep-pens and henhouses. Mrs. Wolf took this as a very good sign.

"Aah, the bloodlust is rising in him," she chortled, rubbing her paws together. "I knew his wolfishness would come out sooner or later."

Towards the end of the three weeks, the weather grew a little warmer, and one day when William trotted through the trees to Septimus' lair, he found that there was no cosy fire waiting.

"Hello, young William," said the old wolf. "I think winter is over, and I'm feeling a little peckish. Let's go and get some breakfast."

Together, the master and the pupil crept down the hill towards the meadow where the new lambs were peacefully grazing. The shepherd boy was chatting to a girl at the bottom of the slope. Thirty plump and pretty lambs grazed sweetly on the green pasture.

"How innocent they look," said Septimus with satisfaction. "Off you go, my boy."

"Go where?" asked William. "I thought we were going to have breakfast together this morning."

"We are! What a sense of humour you have!" chuckled Septimus. "You're going to get it."

"Oh, fine. Where is it?" asked the young wolf, feeling peckish himself now.

"Why there!" Septimus' voice had taken on a sharper note. "The lambs. Look! I should think two each would do to start with. You can always go back for more if we're still hungry."

William was appalled, and he didn't hesitate to say so.

"What? You want me to hurt those dear little woolly things? I couldn't possibly do that. Surely it isn't necessary. I always get my breakfast from my mother. We could go and ask her for some."

Septimus began to look a little more like his reputation. The hair on the back of his neck rose up and his lip curled.

"Where," he snarled, "do you think your mother gets your breakfast from? What did you have this morning?"

"Lamb chops and a couple of eggs," said William promptly. "Ooooh! You don't mean...? She wouldn't...? Not my own dear mother?"

"She would. And she could. And she *did*!" growled Septimus. "And I see now why she sent you to me. Look, it's simple. All you have to do is sneak up to one of those lambs. Grab it round the neck. A quick bite and it's all over. Easy for the lamb. Even easier for you. Got the idea? Off you go!"

Well, William tried. Off he went, sneaking as well as he could (which was a bit loudly). Just as he got near to a plump little lamb, the creature looked up.

William froze. Then his instincts came into play. Not, unfortunately, his wolf-like instincts but his well-brought-up and polite instincts.

"Er ... excuse me," he said. "I'm looking for a spot of breakfast."

A look of alarm crossed the little lamb's face.

"I'm sorry," she said, "I don't think we've been introduced. My name is Lily Lamb. And you are...?"

"William Wolf!" cried the fearsome hunter. "Pleased to...."

But at the word "wolf", the lamb had taken to her heels, calling all her friends to come with her.

"Not," said Septimus drily, "a very promising start. How do you feel about chickens?"

"Delicious!" said William, smacking his lips.

"Then follow me, but be careful not to make any noise. The farmer here is an excellent shot."

"Really? What does he shoot?" asked William pleasantly, as he trotted along beside his teacher. He received in reply a look that would have made your blood run cold. It didn't make William's blood run even remotely chilly.

"Surely not!" he said. "I'm sure no one would be so nasty."

"Shhhh!" The wolves had reached the henhouse.

"There's a nice plump bird sitting just inside the door," hissed Septimus. "Lift up the latch with your nose, dive in, grab her, stop her squawking, and we're off. It's not much of a meal for two but, as you said earlier, you've already had your breakfast this morning."

"Right." William nodded. But he still wasn't sure. "Look, I wonder, is this really necessary?" he asked. "All that squawking, feathers in the mouth, claws in the nose, all that sort of thing. Just for a tiny bite of breakfast. Is it worth it?"

Septimus' reply was brief and to the point.

"Yes," he said.

"Well," William had a brilliant idea. "The thing is, as you can see, I'm new to this sort of thing, and I'm not completely sure about the correct fang position and that kind of detail. What about if, just this time, you show me? I'd be ever so grateful —and so would my mother, I'm sure."

"I'd ... er... love to oblige," said Septimus, "but the fact is, I'm not too keen on chicken really. I pretended to be, to encourage you. It's good stuff for a growing wolf. But I'd just as soon go without, myself. Perhaps we could call in on your mother after all. She might already have lunch on the table."

"Follow me!" called William, mightily relieved that he wasn't going to have to deal with feathers or feet.

Mrs. Wolf smiled broadly when the two wolves appeared at her door.

"Mr. Septimus," she cried, "this is an honour indeed. Please come in. What can I get you? A drink? A little snack? Just a bone to nibble on? I hope my boy has been behaving himself."

"I was thinking more along the lines of a four-course lunch," said Septimus. "We ... er ... we've been so busy this morning working on howling and lurking that we haven't had a moment to stop and get anything for ourselves."

William looked at Septimus. He knew perfectly well that no howling and no lurking had been done, unless you counted five minutes of whispering down by the henhouse. But Septimus gave him a big, special wink, that made William feel suddenly grown-up and proud.

"That's right," he said. "What have you got, mother? That howling is hard work. And as for lurking...."

"Of course it is," agreed Mrs. Wolf, bustling into action. "Just sit down over there, both of you. I've got some lamb, a couple of chickens, and two little piglets freshly caught this morning. I'm sorry there isn't a third, but security is getting very tight down at the piggery."

In no time at all, Septimus was falling upon the meal with undisguised relish. William looked down at his plate and felt a certain queasiness in his tummy. It was hard to feel quite the same about such things when he had seen lambs and chickens hopping about only an hour or so ago.

Once again, William said the first thing that came into his head.

"I'm thinking of becoming a ... what's the word for it? One of those creatures that don't eat meat. Oh, I know. A vegetarian!"

There was a shocked silence in Mrs. Wolf's house. When she spoke again, her voice had taken on an icier tone.

"Is this the kind of talk that you encourage in your pupils, Mr. Septimus

Wolf?" she asked. "Exactly how much benefit has my son been receiving from his lessons with you? William, answer me truthfully, how much killing have you done in the past three weeks?"

"K-k-k-killing?" William sounded appalled. "Why, mother, I wouldn't dream of doing anything like that. It would be cruel. Don't you agree, Mr. Septimus?"

The old wolf shot a look of appeal at his hostess.

"Dear lady, what can I say? I have *tried*. Goodness knows, I have *tried*."

"Really?" Mrs. Wolf's voice was chilling. "So, tell me William, how many creatures have you seen Mr. Septimus Wolf kill in the last three weeks?"

"Oh, mother, I can assure you, Mr. Septimus doesn't do anything like that either," said William eagerly. "Why, he doesn't even like chickens very much."

"That *does* surprise me," replied his mother, eyeing the old wolf's empty plate. "I would have said he liked them very much. Now, Mrs. Septimus, I think that you and I have a small matter of the refund of fees to discuss."

"Dear lady," Septimus shook his head regretfully. "When a pupil is simply not able to carry out the simplest task, it cannot be said to be the teacher's fault. A refund is out of the question, I'm afraid."

"Then I shall have to have a word with the Chairman of the Wolf of the Year Award," said Mrs. Wolf. "I believe it is to be presented next week, but you would know about that better than me, I think."

"This is blackmail!" quavered the old wolf. "Twenty years of ravaging and raging, and this is the thanks I get. So what if a wolf wants to take it easy in his old age? Have a heart, Mrs. Wolf!"

"Your mother," stated William's mother, "ravaged and raged until the day she died. And I begin to think that she's the only one in your family who did, Mr. Septimus. There has always been a lot of talk about you, but now I come to think of it, there's very little evidence that you were ever the fine, fang-sinking wolf you claim. You're a fraud, sir! I'll thank you to leave my table at once!"

William politely showed the visitor to the door. Outside, the old wolf paused.

"Here's a useful piece of advice, my boy. Leave it to the ladies. All that ravaging and raging—they're much better at it than we are. You stick to a little lurking and a lot of good publicity and you'll be fine, just like me."

The other day, I heard of a truly nasty wolf over by the big hill. He goes by the name of William. The stories his mother tells of him would make your brains curdle. She doesn't believe a word of them, of course, but everyone else does, so she's as pleased as punch with her famous son. She says you learn a lot of useful things, listening through keyholes.

The Tiny
Turnip

One day, Meryl's grandfather came to stay. He had recently retired from his job and was finding time hanging a little heavily on his hands. Meryl loved her grandfather, but he wasn't a very exciting person. He had been a bank manager, and although his eyes glowed when he talked about balances and borrowings, it wasn't the kind of thing that interested Meryl very much.

Meryl's mother tried to explain why Meryl didn't really want to spend too much time with him.

"The thing is, Dad," she said as gently as she could, "most eight-year-olds don't really care about pensions. That was why she ran out to play just now, not because she doesn't like you or anything."

The older man looked eager. "But, Dora, they should, you know! Why, if everyone gave a little thought to their future at Meryl's age...."

But his daughter cut him off.

"No, Dad. Tell me honestly, were you interested in banking when you were eight? I know it was a long time ago," she added mischievously.

Her father looked serious. He remembered a little boy with mud up to his knees, helping his own grandfather in the vegetable plot. He could almost smell the earthy odour of the soil as it ran through his fingers. He could see the strong green shoots of the beans as they climbed up their poles. He recalled the sparkling drops of water you could shake from the leaves after a light shower of rain.

"No," he said. "I wasn't in the least bit interested in banking until I was over twenty. But I was lucky, you know. I ended up working in a field that I found fascinating. And it took up all my energy for forty years. The fact is, I don't know anything about anything else. I suppose I should try to develop some hobbies."

"How about making one of them something that a little girl of eight would enjoy?" suggested Meryl's mother. "She would love to share something with you."

That evening, Meryl's grandfather read her a bedtime story.

"You choose," said Meryl, and she tried not to show her disappointment when her grandfather picked out one of the books she had enjoyed when she was much younger. It was the story of the enormous turnip. You remember—a man grows such an enormous turnip that he can't pull it up, and it takes his wife and a cow and a pig and a cat and a dog and goodness knows how many other helpers to get the huge vegetable out of the ground.

In fact, Meryl's grandfather read it rather well, putting in funny voices and sound effects, so that Meryl actually found herself enjoying it.

"I don't think I've ever eaten a turnip," she said sleepily, when the story was over.

"What never?" cried her grandfather. "We must fix that tomorrow."

The next day, Grandfather set off for town with Meryl beside him in the car. "It's not really the right time of year," he said, "but you can buy anything anytime these days, so we should be able to find turnips somewhere."

But the strange thing was, there didn't seem to be a turnip to be had in the whole

place. They found parsnips and swedes and hundreds of carrots, but no turnips at all. Not even frozen ones.

"Never mind," said Meryl. "It doesn't matter."

But her grandfather was not happy. On the way home, he stopped at every farm shop and village store. No turnips. Back at home, he complained to Meryl's mother about the nearby shops.

Meryl's mother frowned. "Dad, this is ridiculous. First of all you couldn't talk about anything but pensions and profits. Now you're obsessed by turnips. Are you feeling well? Maybe you need to get away somewhere."

"I am away somewhere, remember," said her father. "Perhaps it's time I went home, if I can't talk about anything that interests you. After all, I've got to face the future sooner or later. And I *do* have a decent pension!"

Although his daughter tried hard to persuade him to stay, Grandfather's mind was made up. He set off for home the next morning, looking quite cheerful.

For two weeks, nothing was heard of him. Then, one morning, Meryl received a letter. Inside was a tiny packet and a card. It said, "Meryl Sarah Batten Maskovin, I challenge you to a champion turnip contest. The person having grown the largest turnip six months from today will be the winner. Your seeds are enclosed. Good luck!"

In the tiny packet, there were some even tinier seeds. Meryl hurried to find her mother.

"Hmm," said that lady, "so he hasn't forgotten about turnips."

She showed Meryl where to find her gardening books and helped her to dig over a patch of ground at the end of the garden. Then she left her to it.

Once a week, for the next few months, Grandfather telephoned to find out how things were going. When Meryl reported that she had sown her seeds, he said airily, "Oh yes, mine went in last week." When Meryl, with excitement, told him that tiny green shoots were appearing, he said, "Tiny? Oh." When she said that each shoot had two little leaves, he made a tut-tutting noise and sighed, "Only two? Really?" Each week, Meryl came away from the phone feeling depressed, and each week, her mother comforted her.

"I'm sure you are doing just as well as he is," she said, "and anyway, there's still a long way to go yet. He may not get as much sunshine or rain as us in the next few months. Don't worry."

But Grandfather's reports continued to be glowing as far as his own crop was concerned.

"Mine are looking great," he would say. "How about yours, Meryl?"

"Well, they're fine," Meryl would reply, "but I'm not really sure what they're supposed to look like."

Meryl weeded and watered. She thinned out lots of the weaker plants and protected the others from greedy birds and rabbits. Her next-door neighbour put his head over the fence and congratulated her.

"Those are the best-looking turnips I've seen in a long time," he said.

After that, Meryl felt more confident when she talked to her grandfather.

"Good, good," he said. "But are you talking to them?"

"Talking to what?" asked Meryl.

"Talking to the turnips," said her grandfather. "I talk to mine every day. And I play them music, too. It helps them to grow. Only classical, of course."

Meryl discussed the talking-to-plants issue with her mother.

"It can't do any harm, I suppose," was her verdict. "Meryl, does your grandfather sound ... well ... *odd* in any way on the phone?"

"No, he sounds better, really," said Meryl. "Sort of lively. And you know he hasn't mentioned pensions for weeks."

The final day of the challenge came at last. Meryl was up early, making sure her turnips looked their best. At half-past-eleven, a car drew up outside.

Meryl watched through the window as a man got out. She hardly recognized him! Instead of a dark suit, this man was wearing jeans and a sweater. His hair was longer and his face was tanned. He looked well and happy and he walked with a spring in his step, carrying a big bunch of flowers in his arms.

"Where's my favourite gardener?" he cried, hurrying up the front path.

"You look wonderful, Dad," smiled Meryl's mother, as she hugged him.

"These are for you," said her father. "All my own work. I've been doing quite a bit of gardening since I last saw you. As well as other things."

Meryl's mother frowned. "Don't let her be too disappointed, will you?" she whispered. "She has worked really hard, but I think those turnips are pretty average. Tell her she's done well, won't you?"

But Meryl was calling loudly from the back door.

"Hurry up! Come and see my turnips. They look great!"

And they certainly did!

"I know yours will be bigger," said Meryl, "but I'm still quite proud of mine. They're the first things I've ever grown by myself. And it was fun."

"You're a very clever girl, Meryl," smiled her grandfather. "It took me years and years and years to try something new. And you're right. It is fun. But as for my turnips, well, they certainly are absolutely extraordinary. I brought the biggest one along with me."

"Show me! Show me!" cried Meryl. "Is it in the car? Can I go and get it? Or will it be too big for me to carry?"

Meryl's grandfather grinned. "No," he said, "it isn't too big for you to carry. In

fact, it fitted right into my pocket here!"
And he fished out one of the tiniest turnips
you have ever seen!

Meryl and Meryl's mother and
Meryl's grandfather collapsed in laughter
on the path.

"I'm good at growing flowers,"
giggled her grandfather, "but turnips are
not my strong point. I'm afraid I slightly
misled you on the phone."

"I'd say you have quite a talent for fiction," said his daughter.

"Well, it's funny you should say that," replied Grandfather. "That is something else I've been doing. In fact, I've been quite successful. My first story for children is being published next year. It's called *The Tiny Turnip.*

That was some years ago now. Maybe you've read it?